J Haynes

Poems

Respectfully Dedicated to his Friends

J Haynes

Poems
Respectfully Dedicated to his Friends

ISBN/EAN: 9783744770026

Printed in Europe, USA, Canada, Australia, Japan

Cover: Foto ©Andreas Hilbeck / pixelio.de

More available books at **www.hansebooks.com**

POEMS

BY

DR. J. HAYNES.

Respectfully Dedicated to his Friends.

Quebec:
HUNTER, ROSE & COMPANY, ST. URSULE STREET.
1864.

PREFACE.

THE publication of this volume of verses is the result of a number of solicitations from the literary gentlemen of Quebec, with the understanding that they would use their influence in aiding its success and sale.

The Author has published the limited number of five hundred copies, to be circulated among *subscribers only*, in the city of Quebec.

The reader will please observe that a number of songs in this volume have been published, with music, and may be had at Mr. Morgan's Music Store.

The following Ballads, words and music, are by the Author of this volume :—" FAIRY DREAM ;" " WHAT IS HOME WITHOUT A SISTER?" " SWEET EVELEEN ;" " THE MAID OF SYLVAN NOOK ;" "LITTLE CORA'S GRAVE ;" " MY 'NATIVE LAND'S MY HOME ; OR, THE IRISHMAN'S SONG; " and " WHAT IS HOME WITHOUT A BROTHER?"

A number of other Songs in this book have been published with music—the music being by other authors. The poem on the " Southern States " was published in Savannah, Georgia, in 1855, bearing the name of that city. The object now in changing the title is to leave out the part that is purely local, and to adapt it to the general reader.

This volume has been prepared for the press in the midst of the various perplexities of a busy life, and must necessarily bear some marks of imperfection that would not probably have occurred if circumstances had been more favorable.

In conclusion, the Author would not be unmindful of the consideration and encouragement afforded him by the gentlemen connected with the Quebec Press.

DR. J. HAYNES.

QUEBEC, *February* 1, 1864.

CONTENTS.

POEMS.

QUÉBEC.

I LOVE thy quaint old solitudes,
    Where quiet is supreme ;
I love thy towering altitudes,
    And fields of living green.
I love thy gray old moss-grown walls,
    Thy ramparts and their might :
I know their strength when Justice calls
    To vindicate the Right.

I love thy abrupt, craggy cliffs,
    Where eagles love to dwell ;
Thy scaleless mount that always lifts
    Its brow impregnable !
I love thy deathless, grasping hand,
    That holds the nation's key,
Defying armies on the land,
    And navies on the sea !

2

I love thy bright historic leaves,
　　That deeds of valor tell;
For Fame that field with garlands wreathes,
　　Where Wolfe and Montcalm fell !
And Fame their mingled blood will keep,
　　To make two nations one ;
And o'er her sacred urn will weep,
　　'Til pride and envy 's gone.

I love the freedom of thy soil,
　　The heaven-born right of man,
The just reward of honest toil,
　　And God's own glorious plan !
No tyrant shall a sceptre hold
　　O'er thy extended sod ;
No slave for filthy lucre sold,
　　To perish 'neath the rod.

I love thy gay and social scenes,
　　Where hearts and hands are true,
And souls are, like the evergreens,
　　Bedecked with morning dew !
No pageantry thy home beguiles
　　With sin's seductive charms ;
No princely courts, with snares and wiles,
　　And Passion's rude alarms.

I love thy clime and seasons well,
    Though there are softer skies ;
And brighter suns with joy might tell
    Where greater pleasure lies ;
But love's contented with her host,
    Amid the world's great wreck,
And offers up her friendly toast—
    " Impregnable Quebec !"

ART IS ETERNAL.

ERE from the sea of God's unnumbered years
Time's youthful hand had grasped the golden sand,
To drop the atom moments one by one ;—
To measure progress from eternal naught,—
From blind confusion to celestial light
And order ;—ere the sun's effulgent ray
The form of Nature fashioned, Art's regal
Beauty crowned the eternal day of God !

THE GREEN, GREEN LEAVES.

THE green, green leaves of the forest trees,
   Of all sights are the fairest;
And the rustling gay of the woodland bay,
   Of music is the rarest;
They clap their hands in the wide, wide lands,
   While fruits and flowers are growing,
And they shout all day, in the forest gay,
   As summer winds are blowing.

The deep green leaves of the forest trees,
   All speak of life as living;
And their waving sway, and their long, long stay,
   Strong wings to hope are giving:
Not like the flower of a sunny hour,
   They bud and bloom and wither,
And still bid us hope, till the spell is broke,
   And perish altogether.

I love the leaves of the forest trees,
   They speak to me first of Spring;
And in Summer's hour they build me a bower,
   Where I and the wild birds sing.

I weave my wreaths of the green, green leaves,
　That hang on the trees above,
And place on *that* brow, as a sacred vow,
　The pledge of my early love.

The green, green leaves of the forest trees,
　Of all sights are the fairest;
And the rustling gay of the woodland bay,
　Of music is the rarest;
They teach us too, though their words are few,
　And dim our eyes with sorrow,
That we—as they—fall, at Winter's death call,
　And hope a brighter morrow.

ERIN, THE GREENER ISLE.

I'VE seen the palaces of pride,
  And halls of festive glee,
And heard the lute-notes gaily glide,
  As though all hearts were free;
I've seen the pomp of heraldry,
  But these do not beguile :
The better land's beyond the sea—
  The greener, greener Isle !

I've been where perfume fills the air,
  Enchanting every sense;
Where pleasure, love, and beauty rare
  Were not a vain pretense ;
I've been where Nature's hallowed lays
  Were ringing all the while ;
Where hill and valley homage pays
  The greener, greener Isle !

I've seen the trees in beauty bloom
  Where zephyrs softly blew,
And not a shade of verdant gloom
  The flowers ever knew;

I've seen a land where warblers sweet
   The merry hours beguile:
Yet, know I one I'd rather greet—
   The greener, greener Isle!

I've heard the streams with music ring,
   As in the days of yore;
I've heard the chanting ocean fling
   Its anthems to the shore!
I've seen the land where minstrelsy
   The heart could not defile:
That purer land's beyond the sea—
   Erin, the greener Isle!

THE OLD FOLKS.

'T WAS 'neath the honeysuckle's budding gold,
In quaint old chairs of rural fantasy
They sat; and to their children's children told
Fairy stories of their first infancy!
While pretty, peering eyes, with wonder, mute,
In upward glances, caught the trembling tone
That fell like music from a magic flute,
To charm the heart in life's paths sad and lone!

Years had entwined their heads with evergreens
Of sweet contentment; and flowing pleasure,
With rosy sweetness and with dewy gleams,
Had filled their twin souls with heavenly treasure,
'Til their hearts' great spring out-gushed with gladness
At the sweet melody of their own voice;
For age, with hoary hair, brought no sadness
To the heart's reflection, nor to love's choice!

Ah! theirs were snowy locks of second childhood,
All silvered by the hoary frost of time;
Ripened ringlets, by every zephyr wooed,
And verging to a more congenial clime!

The very winds paused in their airy flight,
Their sunny locks to fondle, kiss and toss;
And nodding roses, clothed in summer light,
Their homage paid, before their sweets were lost!

Oh, glorious sight!—old age with virtue clad,
The moral greenery of God's great love!
Two living trees, whose roots and branches had
Withstood the storms of life, and soon, above,
Would be transplanted, to a fruitful soil,
Shaking the soul's great beauties into bloom,
And upward sprouting, without care or toil,
Forever blossom, 'yond the chambered tomb!

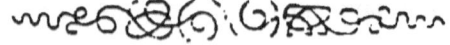

THE YOUNG FOLKS.

Ah! they were spring-flowers, with wreathed smiles,
Flinging the morning glories of their youth
Heavenward; unconscious of weeds and wiles,
That strangle Beauty in her budding truth!
Their mellow hearts, with angel kisses warm,
Made joy more jolly; and the rosy rays
Of their young souls vied with the purple morn,
Nor dreamt they once of sorrow's weeping days!

Their summer life, with bud and orange bloom,
Was in the dreamy future of their hope;
And harvest sickles, reaping for the tomb,
Was all unknown to their bright spirits' scope!
Youth garlanded their brows with peerless joy,
Winging their budding passions into bloom;
And gushing pleasure, without care's alloy,
Saw no sad moments of a future gloom!

Their golden locks, shaking with frolic glee,
Danced in the sunshine of their souls' splendor;
For gray old Time o'er childhood's silver sea
No tempest tossed, bidding peace surrender!

Ah! they were innocent, and pure and bright;
Their hearts with gushing joys and sunny rays
Were thrilled! for life-morn, with crimson light,
Painted the future of their orient days!

Life's summer drought, and autumn's with'ring blight,
Had not yet struck the hope-buds of their years;
And heart-flow'rs, blooming in perennial light,
Were not yet moist'ned with their dewy tears!
Mirth laughed with merry accents, blithe and gay,
And starry love, bedewed with heart-throbs strong,
With wild enchantment charmed their fears away;—
Oh! that their hearts were but forever young!

FRIENDSHIP.

It is a sweet angelic plant,
　　Whose petal eyes weep tears
O'er sorrow, poverty and want,
　　That shade our paths with fears!

It is the dew-lipped fragrant flower,
　　That blooms in genial hearts;
Whose perfume, from its hidden bower,
　　A magic spell imparts.

It is a thornless, blooming rose,
　　By every zephyr kissed;
On which the wilder winds repose,
　　And sigh when it is missed!

It is a flower whose amber leaves
　　Absorb each sunny ray,
And withers not till it relieves
　　The buds that would decay!

THE SPRING IS COMING.

YES, the blue-eyed Spring is coming
   From the balmy, sunny South;
See her sporting, skipping, running,—
   Songs of joy are in her mouth!
See her roll old Winter's carpet,
   White and fleecy, o'er the plain;
Down the mountains see her roll it
   To its frigid goal again.

See her ope the vale of pleasure,
   As with magic's fairy wand,
And restore the hidden treasure
   Winter stole with ruthless hand;
While behind her groves are nodding,
   Nodding in the silver sheen,
And the purple bloom a-dotting,
   Dotting o'er the velvet green.

All around her vocal rivers,
   Piping forth their merry song,
While the gushing streamlet quivers—
   Dancing as it moves along!

3

And a troop of warblers singing
  Notes ethereal o'er the plain;
While the echo music's ringing,
  Ringing in the chorus strain!

Spring is coming o'er the mountains,
  Laughing, frolicking and gay!
See her ope the summer fountains,
  And with roses strew the way.
All around her clouds of glory
  Paint the festooned, fringy trees,
While the youthful and the hoary
  Dance beneath the golden leaves!

Yes, the glorious Spring is coming,
  Breathing now in zephyrs mild,
And the honey-bee is humming,
  Humming anthems strange and wild!
Yet a Spring of greater glory,
  Changing not with months and years,
Waits us, not in song and story
  But among the rolling spheres!

APRIL SHOWERS.

On the meadows and the mountains
  Fall the April pearly showers,
Filling up the crystal fountains,
  Calling forth the summer flowers;
And there 's music in the falling
  Of the soft descending rain,
As the echo sounds are calling
  To the mountain and the plain !

O'er the oceans and the rivers
  Come the dripping vernal showers,
Falling, as the sunbeam quivers,
  On the blooming thirsty flowers;
And the drops in beauty glisten
  On the hillock—o'er the plain,
While the birds, attentive, listen
  To the music of the rain !

O'er the lawn, the field and woodland,
  Come the sparkling diamond drops,
Dancing on the lake and island,
  Spangling o'er the tangled copse !
While above the verdant sprouting
  Of the young and tender grass,
Forest kings with joy are shouting,
  As refreshing showers pass !

MAY TIME.

Spring's heaving bosom, tingling with new life,
　　Feels once again the May-time's warming kiss;
And dread old Winter, with his deathless strife,
　　Recedes and trembles at the new-born bliss.

The sun-kissed waters, like a bird set free,
　　Dip their proud crests and wing to purple isles;
And dancing lakes, shouting with merry glee,
　　To green-eyed fields now fling their wanton smiles.

The very mountains breathe with beauty's glow,
　　As down their slopes the laughing cascades leap;
Babbling amid the greener vales below,
　　Waking the roses from their winter's sleep.

The little hillocks feel the May-time's light
　　Flinging abroad their sweet deliciousness,
And panting fountains from the hill-top height,
　　The peering flowers into being kiss!

WHEN COMES THE SUMMER?

WHEN gorgeous morn, with diamond **dews**,
    Adorns the springing flowers,
And tender buds, with rosy hues,
    Peep through the leafy bowers ;
When fragrant perfume fills the air
    From bloom, for showers longing,
And chirping birds their love declare :
    Then, summer time is coming !

When warblers through the woodland hills
    Their merry songs are singing,
And echo, dell and valley fills,
    And keeps the notes a-ringing :
When shadows lessen in the sun,
    And rivers lowly murmur,
And lakelets by the roses run :
    Then, comes the glorious Summer !

When laughing sunbeams kiss the brooks,
    And dance upon the river,
And zephyrs hide in shady nooks,
    And make the green leaves quiver ;

WHEN COMES THE SUMMER?

When rainbows span the forest hill,
   And thunders softly murmur,
And diamond drops the flowers fill :
   Then, comes the sunny Summer!

When verdant lawn and tangled copse,
   With healing spices breathing,
And tasseled trees their festooned tops
   With emerald crowns are wreathing;
When panting flocks to rivers hie,
   And swains and maids are loving,
And roam beneath the evening sky :
   Then, summer time is coming!

THE SUMMER'S FAREWELL SONG.

FAREWELL! farewell! I am passing away,
    Away to my own sunny South;
I've spangled your hills with violets gay,
    And leave with a song in my mouth.

I floated along on the ether breeze,
    I came with a Nightingale's theme;
And on the high tops of the festooned trees
    I hung up my banners of green.

I breathed on the chilly hills of the North,
    And the ice-bound rivers were free!
I called from the rocks the wild flowers forth,
    Till the valleys all rang with glee!

I've bursted the frozen dells of the earth,
    And clothed with an emerald green
The mountain peaks, from their wintry dearth,
    Till they shouted their verdant sheen.

I've harmonized all the chanting-sea waves,
    And the anthem of each little brook;
And rung a sweet strain from earth's sparry caves,
    And melodized each shady nook.

You know that the dews in each sunny dell
   Are diamonds that drop from my breast;
And the sweet perfume of the heather-bell
   Is my breath on the zephyr's crest.

I love and am loved by each little flower
   That kisses my silvery feet;
And the azure rays, in the lilac's bower,
   Are angels I send them to greet.

I tassel the shrubs in the woodland bays,
   And burst the wild flowers to bloom;
And weave me a garland, spangled with **rays,**
   To beautify yonder sad tomb.

Farewell! farewell! I am passing away,
   Away to my own sunny South;
But I'll greet you again, with lilacs gay,
   And come with a song in my mouth.

AUTUMN.

WELCOME, sweet Autumn! with thy crimson leaves,
   And forest-kings so stately, proud, and sober;
The russet year shall crown your maple trees,
   And mountain songsters chant your mild October.

What pomp and splendor fill the grand old woods
   Of silver beech, of cedar and wild cherry,
When kissing winds breathe through their solitudes,
   And ring the autumn's love song, wild and merry!

The black pine, blasted by the summer gale,
   Like old age, withered by a youthful folly,
Spreads its bare arms to autumn's gentle vale,
   And feels a pleasure in its melancholy.

The mellow clouds of summer's golden hue
   Have softened to a ten-fold deeper glory,
And autumn leaves, still dripping with the dew,
   Repeat again the year's own closing story.

WHEN SHALL I RETURN?

O, WHEN shall I return agàin
    To breathe my native air?
When shall my streaming eyes behold
    Those friends that banish care?
O, when shall I that woodbine porch
    And rustic cottage see?
When shall my soul exult with joy,
    As in the days of glee?

Well, well I knew each winding stream,
    Each brooklet at the door;
Would I were on their grassy banks,
    As in the days of yore!
Would that my hand could pluck the rose
    That withered like my joy!
Would I could cull again the flowers
    I gathered when a boy!

O, when shall I that threshold tread
    That I have tread before?
When shall I see those azure skies
    From out that cottage door?
When shall I cull the gay wild flowers,
    And into garlands twine
To crown my mother's forehead pale,
    While she with love crowns mine?

WEEP NOT FOR THE SUMMER.

WEEP not because the summer's gone,
    With all her wreaths of roses;
Weep not because o'er hill and dale
    The dark brown leaf reposes.
My cottage has its winter flowers,
    Whose leaves are ever vernal :
The smile of childhood's innocence,
    Whose sunshine is eternal.

Weep not because the haggard hills
    By Autumn's blasts are bare;
Weep not because the mountain tops
    Feel Winter's chilly care.
My home has yet the buds of spring,
    Not touched by winter's frost;
No drought hath parched them in their youth,
    No winds their bright locks tossed.

Oh ! happy Maytime ! happy spring !
    With all your dewy store;
You're past, and, like the birds, have flown
    To some bright azure shore !
But, oh ! the joys that you have left,
    With all that's bright and fair,
You've decked our homes with angel smiles,
    With orange-bloom our hair.

Weep not because the summer's gone,
   With all her wreaths of roses ;
Weep not because o'er hill and dale
   The dark brown leaf reposes.
Weep not, for Winter—Death—shall crown
   The youthful and the hoary ;
Shall crown their brows with evergreens
   Of everlasting glory !

DOWN, DOWN, DOWN !

Down, down from your summer's soaring flights,
Down, down from the mountains' chilly blights ;
Haste from the hills to the valleys below,
Old Winter has come with his armies of snow !
      There's shelter I ween
      In the valley's sheen,
      Down in the vale,
      Down in the dale,
      In the home we love,
      From the storms above,
      Happy and gay,
      In Winter's day !

Down, down from the fettered, ice-bound hills,
Down, down from the tempest piercing shrills;
Down, down from the slippery shelving snow,
Down, down where the winter roses grow.
      It 's down in the vale,
      And down in the dale,
      Where gardens green
      In bloom are seen,
      When the hills are shorn
      By the sleet and storm,
      Rugged with care,
      Barren and bare !

Down, down from the flighty heights of pride,
Down, down where the humble saints abide ;
It 's down in the valley—down below—
Where virtue and peace forever flow !
      The summer of life,
      The battle of strife,
      End in the vale,
      Down in the dale,
      Where flowers will wave
      O'er the saintly grave ;
      It 's Summer's last breath—
      The winter of death !

COLLEGE DAYS.

AH! they were hours of life's up-springing rays,
    Gilding the topmost peak of future fame;
Wrapping the soul in dreams of balmy days,
    Winging the hope to grasp a deathless name.

Oh, glorious days!—days of untrammelled bliss
    And gushing glee, from mirth's o'errunning springs,
And flow of soul that friendship stoop'd to kiss,
    Were cherished then as pure and hallowed things.

Life leap'd with joy from hearts that knew no care,
    Flinging with conscious pride each fear away;
Eager to reach, and fortune's battle share,
    And snatch the crown of fame's illusive ray.

Time had not then, with sin's envenomed snare,
    Blighted the blooming hope of budding pride;
Nor conscious guilt, with fearful gloomy care,
    Eclips'd the star of innocence, our guide.

Love swept the string and tuned the heart's sweet lyre,
    Filling the golden hours with regal joy;
And friendship's embers kindled on the pyre,
    Where envy burnt, and jealousy's alloy.

How dreamily the magic moments flew,
  That link'd each hand, and heart to heart in turn;
And all the ties that kindred friendship knew—
  The ties that live in memory's sacred urn!

THE OLD-FASHION FIRE.

You may talk of the comforts of home,
  Your parlors, pianos, settees—
Of the fashions and baubles that foam,
  To dazzle, enchant, and to please;
Of the stove and its heat, when it snows,
  And its pipe that you so much admire;
But for courting, and toasting my toes,
  Why, give me the old-fashion fire.

When the winter and tempests arrive,
  And the gay summer hours are gone;
When the cold, searching winds ever strive,
  And through the drear woods ever moan;
When the labor and toiling shall cease,
  And eve sweeps the strings of the lyre,
And when friendship and love meet in peace,
  Then, give me the old-fashion fire.

How inviting and merry the sight
   Of the old-fashioned chimney-place,
When the firewood laughs and gives light,
   And throws out its arms to embrace !
It is cheering and sweet to behold
   The little ones, whom we admire,
As they laugh at the stories told,
   And sit by the old-fashion fire.

A MAN WITH A SOUL.

THERE 's many good things to admire
   In Nature's extended domain ;
There 's genius and wit, and the fire
   That flashes and leaps from the brain ;
There 's knowledge, and wisdom, and skill,
   And beauty, no choice can control—
But what 's there in Nature can thrill
   The heart, like a man with a soul?

How many have pleasures and mirth,
   And joys and wealth at command,
Who feast on the cream of the earth,
   And build all their hopes on the sand ?

Their garments are crimson and gold,
   And Fashion, she garlands the whole,
While sympathy 's dead and is cold—
   They 've bodies, but not any soul!

A man may be poor and forlorn,
   A destitute creature of earth,
To fame and to fortune ne'er born,
   Nor inherit a title by birth ;
He may not have learning in store,
   Nor wisdom nor wit at his call ;
But yet he is rich evermore,
   If he be a man with a soul!

We love the bright stars of the night,
   And the sun we almost adore,
And the rays of the moon's soft light
   Are blessings we prize evermore ;
But the moon with her silver ray,
   And the sun with his fire at control,
Are eclipsed by the light of the day
   That beams from a man with a soul !

OUTWARD BOUND.

DOWN life's little lake it floated—
  Floated down toward the sea;
And my little bark denoted
  All its native frailty.
Launched from out the deep recesses
  Of the past—the great unknown;
Seaward gliding—leaves few traces
  O'er the river that it's blown!

Soft and stealthy, down the river
  Comes the zephyr—gentle breeze;
Dancing on the wavelet's quiver—
  Wafting us toward the seas.
All life's cares are now in motion,
  Every sail is now unfurled;
Every day brings new commotion,
  As we sail around the world!

Always in the shade or sunshine—
  Sometimes joy, sometimes sorrow;
None have wisdom to divine,
  What to-day—what to-morrow!

Through the whirlwind of life's troubles,
  With a seething tempest round,
Courage counts them all but bubbles,
  When our bark is outward bound!

Calm and smoothly ran the river
  O'er life's little youthful span ;
Still expanding—growing ever,
  Till we reached the years of Man!
Outward bound—o'er ocean's billow,
  Till we reached Meridian's port,
Where the cypress and the willow
  Taught us life was more than sport!

Life's swift voyage is now half ended,
  'Mid the calm and tempest howl ;
Pain and pleasure have contented,—
  Sometimes fair wind, sometimes foul.
Once again our bark is sailing,
  With her timbers staunch and sound ;
Give her one good God-speed hailing,
  For our bark is Homeward bound!

A DREAM OF CHILDHOOD.

Oh! I'm happy, happy, happy!
  I have had a dream of youth;
And I 've scampered o'er the meadows,
  With a heart of love and truth:
I have gathered orange blossoms
  That clustered on each tree;
And I 've heard again the music
  Of humming bird and bee.

Oh! I'm happy, very happy!
  I have found a place of rest,
Like a birdling that had wandered,
  But had found again its nest;
Oh! my heart has leaped with gladness,
  With the depth of feeling stirred,
As I 've listened to the music
  That my spirit only heard.

I have had the sweetest visions—
  The bright visions of life's span;
When the heart was pure and holy,
  Ere it reached the years of Man;

When adown the lake I floated,
  With a shout of childish joy,
When my heart was free and happy—
  I was once again a boy !

But, alas ! it 's but a vision,
  Ere the battle and the strife—
A glimpse of peaceful happiness—
  But a momentary life !
But of all the starry visions
  That come at Memory's call,
The visions of our early days
  Are the sweetest of them all !

THE BROOKLET AT OUR DOOR.

Oh ! 't was sweet to see it scamper,
   Like lambkins o'er the hill;
'T was sweeter still to see it dash—
   A merry, leaping rill;
'T was joy to childhood's bursting glee
   To see it skim the floor
Of rocks and pebbles, grass and weed—
   The brooklet at our door !

And Memory still is vivid with
   My childish, fairy gleam,
As I gamboled to the music—
   The music of the stream.
It seemed the rill was laughing as
   I danced upon its floor,
Clapping its little hands with mine—
   The brooklet at our door.

It rolled along its merry way,
   Kissing the tressy trees;
Flinging its little rougish spray,
   To cool the passing breeze;

'T would breathe a deeper azure blue,
  And waft a living store
To every drooping little flower—
  The brooklet at our door.

And when the spring-morn early decked
  Its way with diamond hues,
The brook with silver lips would kiss
  The dropping pearly dews.
Its limpid depths were sweet and calm,
  Not like the billow's roar,
But gentle as my boyish love—
  The brooklet at our door.

But years have fled, and time has marked
  The sandfall's warning thrill ;
And childhood's sunny hours have fled,
  But not the flowing rill.
I hear its voice,—it murmurs still
  Down in the heart's deep well,—
My eyes are full—its memory 's sweet—
  My little Brook, farewell !

CORA BELL.

"One year ago" they laid her low,
　My darling Cora Bell:
One year ago—too well I know,—
　In humble Primrose Dell.
Chorus—Loving, gentle Cora Bell,
　　　　Sleeping in the Primrose Dell;
　　　　Would my bleeding heart could tell
　　　　Half the love of Cora Bell.

Beneath the hill—beside the rill,
　My Cora Bell doth sleep;
And 'lone with me one willow tree,
　Still weeping, vigils keep.
Chorus—Loving, gentle, &c.

"One year ago" they laid her low,
　While tears like torrents fell;
For all around not one was found
　But loved my Cora Bell.
Chorus—Loving, gentle, &c.

With bitter smart, and broken heart,
　I'll weep in Primrose Dell;
My hopes are fled, my darling's dead,
　Then farewell, Cora Bell.
Chorus—Loving, gentle, &c.

SINCERITY.

O, WHAT a matchless blessing,
　　To feel we are sincere,
To know we 're safely resting
　　On whom we deem most dear !
It is a joy forever,
　　More than we can express,
To feel that nought can sever,
　　Or make affection less.

Life would indeed be dreary,
　　If confidence were lost ;
And none to love when weary,
　　And on life's billow tost !
The soul would sink with sorrow,
　　And loathe the things most dear ;
And dread a coming morrow,
　　If all were insincere.

It is a peerless treasure
　　To have a truthful heart ;
An everlasting pleasure
　　That riches can't impart ;
There 's nothing worth the mention,
　　There 's nought we need to fear,
If, in the world's contention,
　　We find ourselves sincere !

TWO HEARTS.

Vapors that ascend on high,
Spreading out beneath the sky,
Blend their liquid parts again,
As they fall in drops of rain;
Thus in friendship's sympathy,
When two hearts as one agree:
Both will weep in sobs and sighs,
Or with smiling joy arise.

Gushing winds among the trees
Soften to a zephyr breeze,
As they wing each other on,
And by kissing two are one.
Thus the breathing of two hearts
Oft will mingle, till the parts
Lost in love and friendship pure;
And the two as one endure.

Waters, as they pour along,
Often mingle into one;
Streamlets that in mountains be,
Mix and mingle in the sea;
Thus two hearts will often glide
Into friendship's pleasing tide;
Losing their identity
Into Love's immensity.

STEP UPON HER.

Yes, if fallen, step upon her,
   Tread beneath your holy (?) feet,
Though the Saviour fain would save her—
   Though for such the angels weep !
Yet, pollute not your finger
   To uplift when passing by,—
Oh ! ye righteous, let her linger,—
   Trample down and let her die !

Heed not then the secret sighing
   Of that sorrow-stricken soul ;
Though at Mercy's door she 's crying,
   Heed not thou her plaintive call !
Thou art righteous, thou art holy,
   Who can claim thy sympathy ?
Dwell thou on thy virtues solely,
   Proud, disdainful Pharisee !

Tho' her vows and tears be pleading,
   Bidding heav'n and earth to hear,
And to holy thoughts are leading,
   Believe her not to be sincere :

Listen not then once unto her,
   Cast her from thee—far away;
Tho' she claim thee kin and brother—
   Trample on her while you may !

If, in spite of all your graces,
   She sincerely should repent,
And aspire to holy places,
   That her life be better spent;
Then be sure with eyes malicious,
   Keep her 'neath your tyrant will;
Say her aims and hopes are vicious—
   Keep your foot upon her still !

THE LIGHTNING'S SONG.

I LEAP from the clouds in their ebon shrouds,
   And wheel a bright baton of fire;
And dance to the time of the thunder's chime,
   As it rings from its sullen lyre!

I marshal the dire battalions of fire,
   And swifter than light's vivid wings,
O'er mountains I flash, and forest-trees dash,
   And terrify earth's haughty kings!

I leap from the clefts and fathom its depths,
   And strike to the centre of earth;
And blaze on the sky as the seas run high,
   And speed the fierce Hurricane's birth!

I paint, as I fly, with a golden dye,
   The wings of the swift-flying cloud;
And flash o'er the land, 'neath the rainbow's span,
   And the forest-kings rend, so proud!

The darkness and light to my piercing sight
   Forever are one and the same;
And adamant walls, like pure crystal halls,
   I dash through, and tell them my name!

At my wild career men tremble and fear,
  And flee from my fierce shooting ray ;
But harness my fire with triple-cord wire,
  And I'll circle the earth thrice a day !

A hero am I—I stoop from the sky,
  And conquer all distance and space,
And bind without pain, with love's golden chain,
  The hearts of the whole human race !

Each whispering thought my hands have up-caught,
  And over the continents whirled ;
And 'neath the great deep my tongue shall soon speak,
  As I join the old and new world !

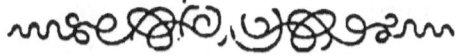

BE GAY.

Be gay, be gay while flowers smile
   In the bright sun's ruddy glow;
Be gay, be gay, and time beguile,
   As the fleeting moments flow!
For cares are light when hearts are bright,
   And short is the life of woe;
Then sing and laugh and pleasures quaff,
   As you merry, merry go!

Be gay, be gay like rosy clouds
   That float in the summer sky;
Be gay, be gay, and Death's dim shrouds
   Shall charm as the rainbow's dye!
For dancing rills, skip by the hills,
   To the merry zephyr's voice,
While blooming trees inhale the breeze,
   And the love-birds make their choice.

Be gay, be gay, for health-blood flows
   When the heart is all a-glow;
Be gay, be gay, for the spirit grows,
   Though the flesh sinks weak and low!

When hearts are strong (though toils be long,
   And the pangs of Sorrow's cup),
'T is heartfelt glee o'er life's rough sea,
   That lifts the spirits up !

Be gay, be gay, for life ebbs fast,
   And falls like a flowing stream ;
Be gay, be gay while youth doth last,
   And hearts with a sparkling gleam !
The joys of life outweigh the strife
   That thick in our pathway hide ;
Then with good cheer outwing all fear,
   As down life' stream you glide !

LOVE'S DOINGS.

LOVE decks the vale and purple hill,
    And clothes the yellow field;
Love makes the rose and vocal rill
    Ambrosial pleasure yield.

Love changes winter into spring,
    And spring to summer days;
Love makes the merry warblers sing
    Their mellow, mellow lays.

Love flings the magic rainbow o'er
    The deep enamelled sea;
Collects her tears in cloudy store,
    And bathes the mountain tree.

Love spreads before the lavish taste
    A thousand summer sweets,
Which, from each hill, and dale, and waste,
    The constant vision meets.

Love makes the clustering stars at eve
    In smiling splendor shine,
And Cynthia silver garlands weave,
    And nature seem divine.

DISPATCH.

DISPATCH !—The spirit's waking word,
   When life to being springs ;
The ceaseless voice of Nature's chord,
   That through life ever rings !
It whispers in the crimson flood,
   As on the current sweeps ;
It echoes to the heart's bright blood,
   As on the torrent leaps !

Dispatch !—The impulse of the tongue,
   The lisping infant's call ;
The living word, the endless song
   That dwells within the soul !
In dreams, it speaks in fairy flow,
   As whispering spirits breathe ;
And lifts above its golden glow
   As our immortal wreathe !

Dispatch !—The hidden, inner life,
   The secret soul of Hope ;
The outstretched hand 'gainst sorrow's strife,
   That with our spirits cope !

It quickens death to life again,
   And from the sullen grave
Leaps forth, the champion to enchain,
   And living banners wave !

Dispatch !—The mainspring of each thought,
   That moves air, sea and earth—
That forth from nothing matter brought,
   And gave all worlds their birth !
Its vital essence thunders trill,
   And with the lightnings race ;
Its vivid powers will ever fill
   Eternities of space !

'T IS WELL WE DIFFER.

'T is well we are not all alike
   In thought, desire and will;
'T is well that objects seldom strike
   Each mind with equal skill!
'T is well that Passion breathes and lives,
   If natural and true;
'T is well that Reason ever gives
   To Right her equal due!

'T is well the seasons come and go—
   The sunshine and the shade;
'T is well that Wisdom made them so,
   And bless'd what He had made!
'T is well that joy and sorrow's cup
   By turns should fill the heart;
'T is well that wealth should lift some up,
   And want make others smart!

'T is well the barren, desert sands,
   The wilderness and waste,
Should differ from the fruitful lands,
   That gratify each taste.

'T is well we find our talents such,
   (If one, or two, or ten,)
Those gifts from Wisdom's golden touch,
   Are gifts the best for men.

'T is well that summer's sun should fill
   Our dells with flow'rs and bloom ;
'T is well that autumn's blight should kill,
   And lay them in the tomb !
'T is well that friends, with sunny smile,
   Should banners o'er us wave ;
'T is well they should our hearts beguile,
   And then pass to the grave !

'T is joy and grief, and want and wealth,
   Bereavement, peace and strife,
'T is wisdom, folly, sickness, health,
   That make the sum of life !
'T is well—though reason seldom sees
   Through passion's sullen mood—
That different talents, taste, degrees,
   Work out the gen'ral good !

6

DIG DEEP.

Dig deep the well in desert life,
  For well is it to know,
'Neath sandy waste and barren heath
  The sweetest waters flow.

Dig deep the weedy, fruitless field,
  It well rewards the toil ;
For 'neath the wasty surface lies
  The rich and fruitful soil.

Dig deep the mine, sink, sink the shaft,
  Far, far beneath the ground ;
For jewels rare and precious ore
  Are 'neath the mountains found.

Dive deep, if you would ever reach
  The richest things that be ;
For purest pearls and diamonds rare
  Sink deep beneath the sea !

Dig deep, for it is well to know
  Whatever 's done or said ;
The greatest things are *to be* done,
  For wisdom lies ahead.

DIG·DEEP.

'T is well to hear, 't is well to know
    What wonders men have done;
But digging deeper soon will show
    New things beneath the sun.

Dig deep—for as the ages roll,
    Philosophy will grow;
Ten thousand undiscovered laws
    The world has yet to know!

Dig deep—but after all you 'll find,
    With knowledge, gold and pelf,
The richest gem is to possess
    Good conscience in yourself!

THE IRISHMAN'S SONG.

SHOULD fortune ever cast my lot
   On some sweet sunny isle,
Where fancy paints a fairy cot,
   And flow'rs forever smile :
Should love's enchanting charms constrain
   My faithless feet to roam,
Yet would my soul with joy exclaim—
   My native land 's my home !

Though foreign dells and foreign hills
   Be ever fresh and green,
And stilly waters, streams and rills,
   Gleam in the silver sheen :
Though foreign friends may kindly call,
   And bid me welcome come,
Yet, it 's the language of my soul—
   My native land 's my home !

If home be but a barren heath,
   And truth and love abide,
It 's better far than 't is beneath
   The palaces of pride.

The heart will linger round the spot,
  No matter where we roam,
And ever sing, whate'er its lot—
  My native land 's my home !

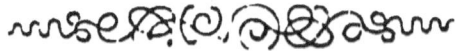

THE OCEAN'S INVITATION.

VISIT, O visit my chambers of pearl,
Down where the fairies and sea-nymphs whirl ;
Down where the nereids and mermaids sing,
Down, down where the musical sea-shells ring !

  My chambers are bright
  With the diamond's light,
  Far down in the sea,
  All glorious and free
  From the storms that pour,
  And the thunder's roar,
  From the lightning's flash,
  And the billow's dash !

Visit, O visit my crystalline halls,
Down by the coral and crystal falls ;
Down by the starry-bright spangled dells,
Down, down by the merry bright laughing shells !

I've mountains of gold,
And jewels untold,
Where coral-leaves curl
In the valleys of pearl,
Where the sea-rose buds
By the amber studs,
All sparkling and bright
In the sapphire light!

Visit, O visit my gold-grotto founts,
Down by the flower-clad silvery mounts ;
Down by the sea-weed's pale velvety sheen,
Down where the vales are eternally green !

I've fairies and fays
In eddying bays,
Who pipe all the day
Their magical lay,
And purple-lined flow'rs,
In crimson-shell bow'rs,
Whose fragrant bloom
The valleys perfume !

TO A MUSICIAN.

I KNOW not the art, nor can I express
   In musical rhythm nor prose,
Thy melodies sweet—but nevertheless
   I 'll garland thy brow with the rose.

I 'll twine thee a wreath of poesy bright,
   And in the great Temple of Fame
In rubies I 'll carve (by the diamond's light)
   Thy musically honored name.

Minerva's sweet flute, with magical tone,
   Might charm and enchant for awhile;
But Apollo's soft lute, by thee touch'd alone,
   Our souls and our senses beguile.

Thy fairy-like strains with harmonic sound
   Will ring in our musical ears,
Till raptures arise as onward they bound,
   To chime with the musical spheres.

A musical charm to the heart bow'd down,
   Is the spell celestial, divine,
That quickens our hopes and makes joy abound,
   And all the gross senses refine,

How earth would decay and mournfully sigh,
  If genius like thine were unknown;
And roses of spring would wither and die,
  And the soul be left sad and alone!

THE BROOK.

A sweet little brook from a shady nook,
  Came forth with a merry song,
And clapp'd its pale hands to the flow'r-clad lands
  As it gently crept along.

It was pure and bright as the diamond's light,
  That sparkles beneath the sea,
And as free from care as the wavelets there
  That roll in immensity!

'T was sprightly and young, and healthy and strong,
  And laughed the gay hour away;
And danced by each hill at the music's trill,
  And kissed the bright flow'rs all day!

And onward it ran, 'neath the rainbow's span,
  Painting itself with the hues,
And frolick'd all day in the rosy ray,
  And from its wing shook the dews!

And life was a gleam of a fairy dream
  To the little babbling brook,
And it kiss'd the branch in its upward glance,
  That shaded the sylvan nook.

For all the bright day the birds piped away,
  And flow'rs in each little nook,
With roguish dark eyes, looked down in surprise —
  Flattered the proud little brook.

But when the dark clouds, in their ebon shrouds,
  Proclaimed the bright season gone,
The birds had all fled, and the flow'rs were dead,
  And the brook was left alone!

But then it was young, and healthy and strong,
  And knew not the pains of strife;
For as it had gone the sun ever shone,
  It thought it could dance through life.

TO AN ARTIST.

THERE 's genius in thy touch,
   And beauty in each line ;
There 's magic in thy brush,
   That makes the art divine !

There life and thought still glow,
   In mimic shade and light ;
There still the passions flow,
   And gracefully unite !

The rosy tinted cheek,
   And sweet expressive eye,
With spirit voices speak,
   As flowers when they die !

And dearest friends of yore,
   (When substance all is gone,)
In shadows speak the more,
   When we are sad and lone !

The hearts we dearly prize,
   That pass from earth away,
We thus immortalize
   In Color's fairy ray !

And though the tongue may cease,
 Our moments to beguile ;
Our love will still increase
 To see their sunny smile!

How pleasant to recall
 The bliss of former years—
The image of their soul,
 Their sun-shine and their tears !

Thus, fading joys of earth,
 We gloriously retain,
And by Art's peerless worth,
 We live life o'er again !

LIFE'S SUNSHINE.

Joys forever are abounding,
    Floating gaily o'er the earth ;
And the inner voices sounding,
    Answer well their priceless worth !
Even in the infant's prattle,
    Mirth in merry accent rings ;
Joyous as the streamlet's rattle,
    Or the bird that ceaseless sings !

Why, then, fret thy soul with sorrow ?
    Sorrow that can ne'er atone ;
Woe that brings a darker morrow,
    Shutting up the soul alone !
Better far to hope and cherish
    Glimpses of a brighter day ;
Faith and Hope will never perish,
    Though they 've but a single ray !

What if friendless and forsaken,
    Will repining aught restore ?
Think ! are all but you mistaken ?
    None that loves you evermore ?
Storms and clouds in life will gather,
    As you battle with the strife ;
But the greater part 's fair weather—
    Look the sunny side of life !

TO A FRIEND.

I DEEM it not a minor thing,
   Along the plains of Life,
To meet some "sunny souls" that sing,
   And banish earthly strife !

Life is at best a rugged path,
   Well strew'd with frowns and wiles;
And hence we prize a merry laugh,
   That through our tears force smiles !

The shades of care will oft increase,
   And wring the heart awhile ;
But, oh ! how soon they calmly cease,
   If "sunny souls" but smile !

The clouds of Night are sad and drear,
   Until the opening Day
Beams forth with splendor, bright and clear,
   And smiles their gloom away !

Methinks it would be sad indeed,
   When sorrow's clouds arise,
If no fond heart our tears could read,
   And smile them from our eyes.

7

And thus I prize a heart like *thine*,
　　Forever bright and gay ;
A soul to cheer, when sad is mine,
　　That shines my gloom away !

THE LOCOMOTIVE.

CREEPING through the cities,
With a stealthy pace,
Panting like a courser,
For the coming race ;
Gliding round the corner,
By the river side,
Shooting through the meadows,
Where the waters glide !

Whirling by the fences,
Whistling at the road,
Puffing o'er the bridges,
Warning all abroad ;

Flying by the hamlets,
Screaming shrill and loud,
Blowing of the whistle,
To a staring crowd !

Spinning through the valleys,
Where the daisy blooms,
Scudding by the streamlets,
And the rattling looms ;
Skipping by the mountains,
Sliding down the grade,
Sweeping o'er the prairies,
With a world of trade !

Dashing through the corn fields,
And the village green,
Slipping by the cascades,
And their silver sheen ;
Brushing by the hillocks,
And the tangled copse,
Humming down the rose-glen,
Decked with diamond drops !

Commerce, with its blessings,
Follow in the *train*,
Wisdom, wealth and goodness,
Labors of the brain ;

Distance, time and places,
All within our reach,
Knowledge flies like lightning,
And Locomotives preach !

A CORRECT MAN.

In Life's rugged paths
　　We seldom can find
A true reliable friend—
　　One manly and kind,
　　Correctly inclined,
That never to pride will bend.

If ever we meet
　　A jewel so bright—
A gem so rare to obtain,
　　We deem it a right
　　To bring to the light,
And his worthy name retain.

Our kind worthy friends
    We all dearly prize,
When true, and all that they seem;
    But to our surprise,
    (Like saints from the skies,)
They are few, and far between!

A faithful, just man,
    Like diamonds rare,
Sheds from himself the true light,
    And all borrow'd glare
    He scorneth to wear,—
His Conscience ever is bright!

He cannot be bought,
    He cannot be sold
For lucre and flattering fame:
    With silver and gold,
    And jewels untold,
You find him ever the same!

THE MONEY PANIC.

THE panic grows, and language flows,
    And fiercer is the strife ;
The money vault is much at fault,
    The main-spring of our life !

What shall we do, when all fall through,
    And Cash gives up the ghost ?
When Millionnaire and ladies fair
    Attend the fun'ral host !

All standing still—the loom and mill—
    It really pierces through !
The people grin without the " tin "—
    Their noses turning blue !

There 's nought to fill a chinkless till—
    The Merchant waits in hope,
And argues well, but cannot sell—
    The Firms and Banks are broke !

It 's so funny without money—
    Quite a serious joke,
When none will lend and Banks suspend,
    And due-bills at you poke !

We strut the town, fly up and down,
    At night we scratch our head ;
Rise in the morn—look quite forlorn—
    Possessing " nary red !"

It 's really strange we have no change,
    Therefore no change can make ;
Will some arrange to make some change,
    That we some change may take ?

We see the end—all must suspend,
    We don't mean by the neck !
Though 't would be right for *those* who might
    Have saved the gen'ral wreck !

We much regret—we 're all in debt—
    We must go up the " spout "—
Insolvent all, as due-bills fall,
    While Commerce has the gout !

FADING FLOWERS.

BEAUTEOUS flow'rs !—God's golden banquet cups,
Flushed in bloom, with fairy nectar filled ;
Tempting the winged bees to tiny sups
Of floral wine, from diamond dews distilled !
Pretty peering pansies with passion pant !
Bursting their mellow hearts with summer glee ;
Kissing the sun-gold shadows as they slant
Adown the azure sky and green-waved sea !

And must they fade away ?　How passing sad
The sound ! how melancholy soft the breeze
With lowly accents whisper ; and the glad
Hum of bees ring lighter through festooned trees !
The very clouds chime forth a solemn tone,
And toll the muffled knell, when flow'rs die ;
Shedding their great heart tears, with sigh and moan,
As scattered roses 'neath their shadows lie !

LIFE—A RIVER.

LIFE's like the shadow of a shade,
  A fog ascending to the mount,—
A misty vapor from the glade
  Distils, and then becomes a fount;
A fount distilled from ether dews,
  From yonder mountain winds its way;
At first it creeps, and then renews
  Its strength with every passing day!

With strength renewed, and joyous bliss,
  Adown the merry cascade leaps,
And smiles at every zephyr kiss,
  As in the flow'ry vale it sleeps!
Refreshed with sleep the wind awakes
  The river from its fairy dream;
And down the wid'ning gulf it takes,—
  The gulf that's widened by the stream.

The sly, the fickle, flirting wind,
  First kiss'd its ripples to assuage,
And then, in anger came behind,
  And roused the river's hidden rage!

With rage and foam, and passion rife,
  The river's settled nature woke;
And in the dashing battle strife,
  The spell of ignorance was broke !

At first the placid, silver stream,
  In peace and purity had flown,
And, in its own ideal dream,
  Its hidden depths had never known;
But when the winds its bosom shook,
  And stirred the deeply-settled lea,
It lost the beauty of the brook,
  And mingled with the roaring sea!

It's thus our mystic life appears,
  A shade, a vapour, then a rill,
A creeping down the vale of tears,
  While subtile snares the passions thrill !
Sleeping, dreaming, leaping, foaming,
  And ever tending to the sea;
Onward ceaseless,—ever moving,—
  Extending to Eternity !

HAVE CHARITY.

THIS world is not what it might be,
   A paradise of love;
Nor is there found that charity,
   That wins a prize above.
We seldom in ourselves can find
   That which we chiefly need—
The magnanimity of mind,
   Which makes us great indeed.

We for our *sect* would rather fight,
   Than for the truth contend;
Would rather conquer than be right,
   And strive the world to mend.
It 's right our silver and our gold
   Should act a goodly part;
But something 's greater, yet untold—
   A sympathetic heart.

Give me a soul that will disdain
   All party creeds and show;
A soul that never will refrain
   To sympathize with woe:
A heart and hand for every tear,
   No matter in whose eye,
May stand that signalizing fear,
   And offspring of a sigh.

MY GARDEN IS THE WORLD.

I HAVE a garden with an endless walk,
With statues, urns, and flowers that strangely talk;
With fountains, cascades, and some prattling brooks,
And fish, and birds, and many sylvan nooks!

Here are all trees that deck the forest gay,
And hills, and dells, where hide the beast of prey;
Likewise broad rivers, on whose silver streams
Dance golden rays in summer's ruddy gleams!

Here are inland seas, which to the ocean
Resistless rush; while their mad commotion
By mountains mighty, impetuous dash,
'Til waves tumultuous give lash for lash!

And here prodigious caves' deceptive sound,
Where ghostly echoes vibrate and rebound;
And winged shadows, flitting speechless by,
Moan through the winds and murmur to the sky!

Also gigantic cliffs, on whose abrupt crags
I, like the eagles, soar, till fancy flags
And wings to milder scenes—to mossy rocks—
To laughing lakes—to rills, and bleating flocks!

This garden 's made imagination free,
And winged my fancy with the honey bee,
To every am'rous vale of flowers, and streams,
And made me mad with pleasure, love and dreams!

I 've wandered here in twilight's holy hour,
When sparkling diamonds decked the festooned bower;
And quiet Eve crept o'er the rosy hue,
And noiseless scattered gems of pearly dew!

I 've watched its tender buds, and bloom and fruit,
And heard its songs, and sighs, and I 've been mute
As night-shade phantoms danced among the leaves,
And dying zephyrs trembled through the trees!

In this strange garden I have often walked,
And with its flowers, and trees, and birds have talked;
Have sought its windings and its lab'rinths wild,
With tears of joy and wonder, since a child!

And these have been my churches, teachers, schools,
Whose inspirations deep have taught me rules
And laws divine, and universal love,
Whose quenchless flames have borne to joys above!

8

And I have thought, with contemplative mind,
The *world* a *type*—reflecting forth mankind—
The beauties, wilds, and fancies of the heart;
Our hopes and fears—and is our *counterpart!*

OUR DAILY DUTY.

Ls t for the things that perish,
　　Man should only slave and toil
And his daily wants replenish,
　　By the tillage of the soil?
Is the clattering of the mill,
　　Voices only that may call?
Is it at the loom and anvil,
　　Graver duties daily fall?

No! there 's something sweet and softly
　　Speaking to the soul of man;
Prompting him to things more lofty
　　In life's concentrated plan!
Daily duties, high and holy,
　　Far above all other kind,
Are the acquisition solely
　　Of the heart, and soul, and mind!

Truth and friendship are the beauties,
　　Beauties that adorn the heart;
Love and goodness—these are duties,
　　Duties of a higher art!
Riches great and peerless beauty,
　　Thousands covet while they live;
But ambition's noble duty
　　Is the learning to forgive!

Well to heed our daily calling,
　　And for present wants provide;
Never as the sluggard falling
　　Into filth and folly's pride!
Heart and soul (while hands are plying)
　　Should some good for others plan;
Minds magnanimous are trying
　　To improve their fellow-man!

THE DYING SUMMER.

DYING Summer 's gently gliding
    Into Winter's frigid grave,
While the falling leaves are hiding
    Beauties that around her wave.

Still are gems of beauty glowing,
    As the grove she tesselates,
With the floral wonders growing,
    Wonders that her life creates.

Rich and gorgeous is the pillow
    Where she lays her dying head,
'Midst the gold-fruit ripe and yellow,
    And the flowers blue and red !

Happy Summer, bright and airy,
    Brilliant, transient—linger still ;
With thee, life and fay and fairy
    Vanish all from mount and rill.

Roses sweet with dew-drops weeping,
    Woo thee lovingly to stay;
Stilly streams and cascades leaping,
    Bid thee not in haste away.

Laughing hours of sunny gladness,
   Fall-winds still will blow away;
Leaving leaves to sigh in sadness,
   As they wither day by day.

While the sultry Autumn 's breathing
   Perfume from each dewy flow'r,
Summer's hand is gently wreathing
   Garlands for her parting hour.

Youthful June and July glories,
   With their beauties pass away;
Serve but as " *Memento Mories* "
   Of all pleasures bright and gay.

KICK HIM DOWN.

IF in the treach'rous path of life
   Thy brother's foot should slip,
And words of folly, hate or strife,
   Fall from his thoughtless lip;
Or if perchance, as many say,
   Dame Fortune she should frown,
And blight his prospects, fair as day,
   The cry is—kick him down!

What'er his state in life has been,—
   If honest, worthy, wise,—
Or if the wealthy day hath seen,
   Of course you'll shut your eyes.
If poverty, with brazen chain,
   Should bind him to the ground,
And struggling, 'tempt to rise again,
   The cry is—kick him down!

If solitude and penitence,
   For errors be his lot,
And conscience brings remembrance
   Of follies once forgot;
If hope again with buoyant wing,
   Flings joy and peace around,
A thousand accusations bring,
   And try to kick him down!

If on his well-meant efforts rest
  The helpless child for life,
And near his doubting, beating breast,
  There hangs an anxious wife;
If on the altar of his care
  Their hopes and joys are bound,
What retribution waits your share,
  Who aid to kick him down?

If good intent the man should guide,
  Though failing in a part,
Discourage not—the world is wide—
  There 's good in every heart.
Let sympathy the soul inspire,
  Where'er misfortune 's found,
And man still struggling up admire,
  And never kick him down!

UNSEEN TEARS.

UNSEEN tears are like a river,
　　Springing from the mountain high,
Gliding noiseless—flowing ever—
　　Hidden from the gazing eye.
None may mark the tear-drop starting
　　From affliction's bitter smart ;
None may heed the hope departing
　　From the broken, bleeding heart.

When alone in silent sadness
　　Comes the heart-felt gushing tear,
Quenching every ray of gladness—
　　Quickening every anxious fear :
Then indeed we feel the sorrow,
　　Bursting from a soul of woe—
Shadow of the gloomy morrow,
　　Growing darker as we go.

Heart-felt anguish is retiring
　　From the world's unhallowed eye ;
Solitude to grief's inspiring,
　　Freeing every struggling sigh.
Thus the spirit bears the wringing
　　Sorrow brings in dreary tone,
While our ceaseless cares are bringing
　　Countless fears, because alone.

'T is within the soul's recesses,
　Deep and hidden from the view,
Where the heart-pang closely presses,
　Smiting every vital through.
When the raging flame of sorrow
　Boils the caldron of the heart,
Scalding tears will reach the furrow,
　And the eyelids feel the smart.

Could we see the *inner* weeping
　Of the dark, despairing soul,
Think you we 'd neglect the keeping—
　Or unheed our brother's call ?
But, alas ! the world is telling
　Startling things of human woe,
While ten thousand hearts are dwelling
　On the griefs but *One* can know.

WHAT THE ANGELS DO.

THEY bid the bright sun on his journey to run,
  And show the great monarch the way;
And the chargers of fire that ne'er weary or tire,
  They bind to the chariot of Day!

Then open are borne the gold gates of the morn,
  Unlocked by the Angel of light;
And the first ruby ray with joy heralds the day,
  And chases the clouds of the Night.

They teach the young bird the first notes that are heard
  In the valleys that merrily ring;
And they gaudily dye, with the tints of the sky,
  The fairy-like butterfly's wing.

The sweet zephyr's breeze, by the young blooming trees,
  That fans in the gay summer morn,
Is the solace they fling from their soft downy wing,
  To the flowers, as soon as they 're born.

They gather the dew from the roseate hue,
  That paints the bright amorous sod,
And in goblets of gold, as the ancients of old,
  They quaff to the great Day-God!

From oceans and streams, by their bright, lurid beams,
   They bid the moist vapours arise,
Then thunder aloud through the water-charg'd cloud,
   Till pearly drops fall from the skies.

And in the gay race through ethereal space,
   They guide the great chariot of Day ;
And the curtains of Night they roll up in their flight,
   And dark, dusky clouds fan away.

The crystalline towers in their aërial bowers,
   They sprinkle with diamonds and pearl ;
And the purple-tint sky they adorn as they fly,
   And their banners of gold unfurl.

As onward they run with the luminous sun,
   They pluck down each glimmering star ;
And the ether-gold beams with the sun's brighter gleams,
   They fling from their sapphire-like car.

The blue firmament they spread out like a tent,
   And rainbow it down to the earth ;
And they crimson the West with the rays of their breast,
   When Day gives to Night her dark birth.

A ruby-bright bed for the sun's brighter head,
   They spread for the monarch of day ;
And with curtains of gold they his glory enfold,
   And shut up the last burning ray.

The young timid Night they lead forth to the light
   Of Luna, and Venus and Mars ;
And they banish her fears as they tune the gay spheres,
   And spangle her robes with the stars.

TO MRS. L. H. SIGOURNEY.

I saw her in the evening
   Of Life's uncertain course,
With the fire of genius beaming
   From the soul's unsullied source ;
And around that brow majestic,
   The loving smile would play ;
And the heart seemed more elastic
   With virtue's burning ray !

I saw her in the evening—
   Her race was nearly run,
But the Lamp of Life was gleaming
   With glories she had won ;

And still that voice was ringing,
   Like music wild and free !
While holy thoughts were winging,
   As fleece clouds o'er the sea !

I saw her in the evening—
   Life's cares had passed away,
But not without their weaving
   A chaplet bright as day !
For round her path were streaming
   The rays of joy divine,
And brighter still were beaming
   The hopes that inward shine !

I saw her in the evening—
   Life's battle she had fought ;
And fame her brow was wreathing
   For poesy's bright thought !
For in her train—excelling
   Ten thousand voices strong,
The chorus notes were swelling,
   To crown her Queen of Song !
9

SPRING VOICES.

WHISPERS sweet in softest cadence,
    Fall enchanting on the ear;
Breathing gently in the radiance
    Of the sun-beam, bright and clear!
Music murmurs faint and lowly,
    From the river's plaintive song;
Dreamy voices sounding slowly,
    As the waters move along!

Voices gaily ever singing,
    Singing through the budding flow'rs;
Infant voices ever ringing
    In the merry sunshine hours!
Sounds that echo in the morning
    Speak the spring-time rosy light,
While the leaves the trees adorning,
    Speak the passing winter night!

Laughing roses ever greeting
    Ears attentive on the way;
Blooming lilies ever speaking
    In the sunny joyous ray!
Wisdom-voices ever calling,
    Speaking by the sprouting grass;
Tones of gladness ever falling,
    Falling as the thoughtful pass!

Every field, and plain and mountain,
　　Echo with the vocal sound;
And the upward gushing fountain
　　Bids the joy of spring abound!
Speaking-voices ever swelling,
　　As the leaves by zephyrs nod;
Stilly voices ever telling
　　Of the goodness of our God!

GENIUS *VS*. CIRCUMSTANCES.

I KNEW a man not long ago,
　　A man of virtues rare,
Who never to a school did go,
　　Or prayed *in church* a prayer.
To classic lore of ancient day
　　He was not much inclined;
Of Greek and Latin, not a ray
　　Did e'er illume his mind.

With snobbish pride, to learned wit
    He never made pretence;
And affectation, he thought it
    Beneath his common sense.
And yet, he never did despise
    The learning or the learned;
But over woe, with weeping eyes,
    From day to day he mourned.

His nature was both kind and true,
    With little wealth or power;
Yet he knew more than sages knew,
    For every trying hour.
Yet, dim his sun in cloudless days,
    And weary he had grown,
For others' grief obscured the rays,
    And folly not his own.

No creed or party he espoused,
    But for the truth would fight—
A valiant hero, when aroused
    To battle for the right.
He was a leader firm and bold,
    And artless as a child;
To sordid lucre ne'er was sold,
    Nor to fanatics wild.

His life was great, as was his soul,
   Magnanimous and good—
No party zeal—but for the whole—
   The gen'ral welfare stood.
He could not boast of learning deep,
   Yet much had he in store:
A mind to know, to feel and weep—
   A genius—though was poor !

THERE 'S GOOD IN EVERY HEART.

TELL me not in doleful accent,
   Human nature has no good;
Though in folly comes its advent,
   And its demonstrations rude.

Tell me not in bitter sadness,
   Man 's corrupted through and through;
That his nature runs to madness,
   Thoughtless as to what may do.

Tell me not there 's no aspiring,
   Native, genuine and true;
That no innate spark 's inspiring,
   Common both to me and you.

Tell me not in plaintive cadence,
  Man 's the meanest on the sod;
While around his brow the radiance
  Speaks the image of his God!

Wilful folly, deeds revolting,
  Are exceptions—not the rule;
Nature ever is exalting—
  Teaching wisdom by the fool!

Though the soul be often falling
  In with sin's alluring mood,
Yet are inward voices calling—
  Nature will approve the good!

Wiser then it is to ponder
  On the wide world's better part;
Nor will wisdom ever wonder
  That there 's good in every heart!

THE FAIRY DREAM.

I SLEPT in the halls of crystal space,
  And spangled me o'er with stars,
And curtained me with the rainbow's wing,
  As it stood on its airy spars.
'T was then in beautiful dreams I saw
  The land of ethereal air;
And heard the sweet song of fairy elves,
  As they played with my golden hair.

I slept in the halls of crystal space,
  On clouds of ethereal gold,
And pillowed my head in crimson red,
  And dreamed of the glories untold.
I dreamed of the elves and fairies bright,
  That flitted on gossamer wing,—
Of amber, and rose, and sweet repose,
  And birds that eternally sing.

I slept in the halls of crystal space,
  And wrapt me in purple and blue,
While elves, at my head, painted my bed
  With the tints of the rainbow hue.

I dreamed of the friends of childhood's years,
   Of lovers, and joys that are past,
And saw them all there in realms so fair,
   That spring doth eternally last!

I slept in the halls of crystal space,
   And spangled me o'er with stars,
And covered me with the rainbow's wing,
   As it stood on its airy spars.
I slept, and I dreamed—joys that will fill
   The soul with great pleasure for years—
That those whom we love meet there above,
   And chant with the musical spheres!

ON A GIFT-BOOK FROM A FRIEND.

TEN years ago, well, well I know,
　　When first as friends we parted,
From you I took a little book,
　　As tear-drops downward started !
" If I would roam far, far from home,
　　To tarry with the stranger,"
You said—" 't would heal the pains I 'd feel
　　From envy, scorn and danger."

With mournful look I took that book,
　　(A prize beyond all measure,)
And o'er it wept, and safely kept
　　It as a " sainted " treasure !
And still it lives, and ever gives
　　(Whatever my condition,
If tears make sad, or hopes make glad,)
　　Its silent admonition.

Years, years have fled, old friends are dead,
　　Old friends I well remember ;
Nipp'd in their prime, by cruel Time,
　　As flowers in December.

And stealthy age has strewed life's page
  With sunshine, tears and sorrow;
And still content, my hours are spent—
  Hope sees a sweet to-morrow.

This book, I think, contains a link,
  A link that bound together;
It seems each leaf is but a brief,
  That we should sever never.
O'er all life's sea, this book to me
  Has been a guide and brother;
A trusty friend, his aid to lend—
  I love it as no other.

KNOW THYSELF.

" KNOW then thyself," a maxim old,
  By sage and prophet taught,
An antiquated precept told—
  By dear experience bought.

" Know then thyself," in golden light
  On Delphos' temple shone,
And by the god Apollo's might,
  It sparkled from his throne.

" Know then thyself" in early life,
  Ere folly blind thine eyes;
Adjust the balance, face the strife,
  And win the glorious prize!

" Know then thyself" in riper years,
  When fickle fortune smiles,
And golden lucre charms thy fears,
  With fascinating wiles.

"Know then thyself," should flat'ring fame,
  With silver trump declare
The transient glory of thy name—
  A bubble in the air.

" Know then thyself," by every rule,
　In nature, science, art,
The wise man be, and not the fool,
　Who trusteth his own heart.

" Know then thyself" in every lane
　Of busy, restless life ;
Thy talents, glory, and thy shame,
　And Death's unfailing strife.

HOW FREE LOVE CAME.

Now Free Love came to my window pane,
    As oft as he passed by ;
With lifted hat, and a rat, tat, tat,
    And winking, leerish eye.

With a pat, pat on my morning cap,
    And a chuckle 'neath the chin,—
With finger whirl at my long black curl,
    He tried my heart to win.

I knew his smiles and his wanton wiles,
    And flattering tales to me ;
With his rat, tat, and his chit, chit, chat,
    And heartless love so free.

And still he came to my window pane,
    I knew no reason why ;
But saw deceit in the way he 'd meet
    The glances of my eye.

" I 'm free ! I 'm free in my love," cried he,
    " Each equal joy I bring ;
Then take a part of my full, full heart,
    Free Love 's a glorious thing."
10

" That 's all my eye," was my short reply,
   " Your love is much *too* free;
With your pat, pat, and your chit, chit, chat,
   You will not do for me."

So off he fled, with his empty head,
   For plainly could I see,
Though love his name, and he often came,
   Yet no *true* love had he.

IT 'S NOBLE TO FORGIVE.

Though the nature we inherit
   May to dreadful deeds inspire,
And our foes may justly merit
   Envy's rage and fiercer fire :
Yet, it 's nobler far to cherish
   Thoughts of friendship while we live—
Letting angry feelings perish,
   And forgiving, still forgive.

What if vice and bitter slander
   Cloud the brow and flame the heart ?
Is it wise in hate to ponder,
   And by brooding feed the smart ?
No! when raging malice flashes,
   Bidding every passion live,
Bury it in Reason's ashes,
   And forgiving, still forgive.

Nought but charity will cover
   All the seeming griefs of life,
And with wings of mercy hover
   O'er the heartless world of strife.
Noble then it is to cherish
   Thoughts of friendship while we live—
Letting angry feelings perish,
   And forgiving, still forgive.

SHE 'S A MODEL.

I SING not of her faultless form,
    Not of her Grecian face,
Not of those lips that breathe so warm,
    Of concentrated grace.

I sing not of her peerless eye,
    That laughs in seas of love,
And shames the cloud-empurpled sky,
    And cherubs feast above.

I sing not of those tresses fair,
    That cluster like the vine,—
Those raven ringlets, jet black hair,
    That deck a head divine.

I sing not of her classic nose,
    That Venus would adorn,
Those pearly teeth and lips of rose,
    And cheeks like tingy morn.

I sing not of those tiny feet,
    That make enchanted ground,—
Not of those fairy fingers sweet,
    That angels cling around.

I sing of something rarely seen—
  A model *head* and *heart ;*
Beauty and love are fixed within,
  Which Death can only part.

LAUGH ON.

WHY should sullen clouds of sadness
  Frown upon thy youthful face ?
Why, when summer's joy and gladness
  Smiles and breathes in every place ?
Time enough for sobs and sighing,
  When life's pleasures are all gone ;
But while these remain undying,
  Nature's cry is, laugh, *Laugh On !*

Why should timid hearts stand blushing,
  Fearing, lingering on the plain ;
While the merry streams are gushing,
  Dancing to the goal again ?
Time enough to fear life's troubles,
  When unfriended and alone ;
But when trials are but bubbles,
  Let them pass, and still *Laugh On !*

Why those downcast eyes, despairing,
  Withering care and chilling looks,
While the lily blooms uncaring,
  Smiling by the laughing brooks?
Time enough to fear the wringing
  Sorrow brings in dreary tone;
But while summer birds are singing,
  All their music says, *Laugh On!*

Why despond, when songs of gladness
  Echo through the forest trees;
When no moaning zephyr's sadness,
  Sighing through the verdant leaves?
Time enough—for life is wasting,
  Bid it not in haste begone;
Urge it not—'t is quickly hasting,
  To retain it, laugh, *Laugh On!*

"Look aloft," when thoughts are swelling,
  Bursting every heart-felt tie,
Listening stars your fears are telling,
  Wafting them beyond the sky!
Vex not then thy heart with sorrow,
  Sigh not then in mournful tone;
Think not of the coming morrow,
  While you live, I say, *Laugh On!*

HUM-BUGS.

To speak of hum-bugs great and small,
   I must all sails unfurl,
And circumnavigate the globe,
   And visit all the world.
But as no reason could expect
   Such an extensive call,
Permit me just to name a few—
   A picture of them all.

Some bugs there are that always hum,
   And some are all humbug,
Who never hum, but bear-like come,
   And close their victims hug.
Some bugs are larger than the rest,
   And rotten to the core;
We call them " big-bugs," 'cause they suck
   The life-blood of the poor.

The statesman he 's a bug that hums,
   If not a great humbug;
For sure he wins by good " soft-soap,"
   A sum both safe and snug.

The lawyer, too, is not behind,
  He " up to snuff " will come,
And take his share, while bugs prepare
  To quarrel, fight, and hum.

The doctors all act well their part,
  They hum as well as sting ;
May ease your head with pills of bread,
  But down your cash they 'll bring :
Or if to nostrums you 're inclined,
  (And ten to one you are,)
You 'll soon get lean while they get fat,
  And all the better fare.

Of course the merchants never hum,
  But sell below the cost,
Tremendous sacrifices make,
  And live well by the lost !
'T would be severe to tantalize,
  Or even to suggest
That those do not stick to the truth,
  As well as all the rest.

You never heard mechanics hum,
  I 'll bet they never do ;
But still, somehow, they learn " to come
  The putty " and the glue.

Of course the printers we except,
   And all the world knows why ;
For should I here declare they hum,
   They 'd knock *this* into *pi !*

The farmers only we excuse,
   Bugs less disposed to hum,
Though well the *words* express their traits,
   When they to market come.
The ladies all we *must* pass by,
   For they are pretty things ;
And though they hum occasionally,
   It 's just to show their wings.

Thus all the world 's a humbug show,
   (Though all the world protest) ;
'T is true we sometimes find a few
   Less guilty than the rest ;
But all, at times, when facing right,
   Will knowingly deceive,
Assenting by our words and looks,
   To what we ne'er believe.

THE DIGNITY OF DOLLARS.

A NOBLE heart is not the part
    That will affect our standing;
And to behave with knowledge grave
    Is not at all commanding.
A worthless fool may sit and rule,
    Provided he 's the coffers,
And all see then as wiser men,
    The dignity of dollars!

When wise men prate on church and state,
    On order, law and morals,
They think the dimes (in better times)
    The very best of laurels!
The old and young, the weak and strong,
    In love or matrimony,
Know well the might, and wrong or right,
    Go strongly for the money!

If ere we meet in converse sweet,
    And tales produce their thrillings,
We must fill up the pleasure cup,
    With pennies, pounds and shillings!
We still persist and will enlist
    Religion with the money!
It 's not enough to get a bluff,
    For etiquette so funny;

The loom and mill, and grocer's bill,
   Are always weighty matters ;
But not the poor, who at your door
   Stand clothed in rags and tatters !
The preachers now will often bow
   To luring Lucre's colors ;
And sell the soul, and pray for all
   The dignity of dollars !

To make a show the best will " blow,"
   And even now the papers,
However strange, to get the change
   Will cut some funny-capers !
There 's Fashion's imp, (a lordly " pimp,")
   All fancy vest and collars,
Will puff and swell and loudly tell
   The dignity of dollars !

We read of times, in prose and rhymes,
   About the golden ages,
When minds were fed and men were led
   By wise and truthful sages ;
But what, alas ! has come to pass ?
   A substitute for scholars,
For all maintain and loudly claim
   The dignity of dollars !

I 'LL NEVER SAY FAREWELL.

To thee I ne'er can say farewell,
    My happy home, my native land;
Chain'd by love's undying spell,
    I ne'er can shake a parting hand.

To thee I ne'er can bid adieu,
    Where'er I roam, where'er I stray ;
Tho' drinking Eden's nectar dew,
    Thy presence flits across my way.

Oh, no ! I ne'er can say good-bye,
    Tho' Paradise should me surround,
And all the music of the sky,
    Yet would I love thy hallow'd ground.

No, no ! I ne'er will say farewell,—
    No friend nor foe shall me beguile ;
I 'll praise thy tranquil shores, and tell
    The magic of thy sunny smile.

Should e'er thy friends unfaithful prove,
    Should all thy foes thy freedom sell,
From thee my soul should never move ;
    I 'll die—but never say farewell !

PEACE-MAKERS.

THERE can, in this vile world, be found
Some little spot of happy ground,
Where village pleasures flit around,
   Without the village tattling !
And doubly blest that spot must be,
Where Love sits crown'd by Liberty,
Free from the bitter misery
   Of scandal's endless prattling.

And such a spot is really known,
Where Dame Peace claims it as her own ;
And in it she has fix'd her throne,
   For ever and for ever !
There, like a queen, she reigns and lives,
Where each the other's fault forgives,
The little slights that each receives,
   And are offended never.

No mischief-makers there remove
Far from the heart that warmth of love,
Which leads us all to disapprove
   What gives another pleasure.
11

None seem to take one's part—and when
They 've heard their cares, unkindly then
Run and retail them all again,
    Mix'd with their poisonous measure.

None seem to have the cunning way
Of telling ill-meant tales, and say—
" Don't mention what I' ve said, I pray,
    I would not tell another."
They never to your neighbor go,
Narrating everything they know,
And break the peace of high and low—
    Wife, husband, friend and brother.

None act the sad, degrading part,
To make another's bosom smart,
And plant a dagger in the heart
    Whom they should love and cherish.
In this bright spot is always found
Peace and good-will with all around,
While friendship, joy, and love abound,
    And angry feelings perish !

If you would find that happy spot,
Go search in yonder woodland cot,
Where God has bless'd the poor man's lot,
    And fill'd his heart with pleasure!

There, in that rural, sweet retreat,
Where artless smiles each other meet,
Peace-makers you may always greet,
For God is their great treasure.

I WOULD I WERE A FAIRY.

I WOULD I were a fairy fair,
   I would not dwell in forest dell,
Where thunders rend the summer air,
   And mountain trees their terrors tell.

I would not haunt the watery waste,
   Where raging seas and billows roar,
Nor scale the craggy rocks, nor haste
   To scan the wild and boundless shore.

I would not, o'er the barren heath,
   To thirsty plain and desert fly,
Nor linger where no garland wreath
   My brow would deck in summer sky.

I would I were a fairy bright,
   I 'd dance on every bubbling brook;
I 'd wing to syren-isles of light,
   And chant in every sylvan nook.

I would I were a fairy bright,
   I 'd sport and gambol with the wind;
I 'd dwell in yonder gold cloud light,
   Where bright-eyed stars like diamonds shine.

I would I were a fairy fair,
   I 'd sleep on clouds of downy gold;
I 'd build my house on ether air,
   And watch the silver moon to roll.

I would I were a fairy bright,
   I 'd dwell with Venus, goddess love;
I 'd sing to peerless stars of night,
   And hymn the rolling spheres above.

RISE EARLY.

Up! up and away,
And meet the dizzling ray
    Of Apollo's car,
    That shines afar,
When Aurora opes the day.

Up! up and away,
Rise at the break of day,
    To the merry fields,
    And laughing hills,
In the sun's bright gentle ray.

Up! up and away,
No longer slumb'ring lay;
    For the rosy sky,
    In purple dye,
To the mountains bid you stray.

Up! up and away,
Wake at the vocal lay
    Of the mocking bird,
    And bleating herd,
In the sun's bright golden ray.

LOVE ME WHILE I LIVE.

THE adage of old is true I ween,
   That "we live not till we die;"
That virtue and worth cannot be seen,
   'Til we reach the Courts on High!
Temples of pride and pillars of fame
   Are glories that mortals give;
But what are the joys of pomp and name,
   If you love me while I live?

The evergreen wreaths that may crown you when
   In the grave you lie your head,
Will not be pleasures you joy in then,
   When the vital spark has fled!
Then muffled drum, the shouts of host,
   The praises that sound so high,
Are not the blessings mortals need most—
   You should love them ere they die.

A DREAM OF LIFE.

I DID not dream of pleasures
   Voluptuous and gay,
As back life's path I scampered,
   In visionary play ;
I saw no gold-tip'd temples,
   In retrospective view,
That I had seen in childhood,
   When life's morn dripp'd with dew.

I saw no starry blossoms,
   In clusters on each tree ;
I saw no budding flowers,
   No winged honey-bee !
I heard no songs of glory,
   No music wild and free ;
I saw no forms of beauty
   That once enchanted me !

I sighed, as down the vista
   I cast my wond'ring eye ;
That forms so beauteous and fair
   Should wither, sink and die !
I sighed, till vision failed me ;
   Then came *another* dream,
And beauties down the vista
   Were brighter than I'd seen ;—

The fairy dreams of childhood,
  The love, the peace, the smile,
And the joys of innocence
  That infant hearts beguile;
The holy ties of friendship,
  The pure and virgin love,
Came back with reminiscence
  Of a purer life above!

And thus the visions taught me
  That nought can live in vain;
Though blooming flow'rs disappear,
  'T is but to come again;
That thoughts of love and beauty,
  With every fairy dream,
Will flow and spread forever
  In one eternal stream!

LIGHT—THE PICTURE REALM!

On, fairy realm of undiscovered bliss!
    Whose forms are fancy, fleeter than a ray;
Whose shoreless seas with joy forever kiss
    The streaming light that fills eternal day!
How infinite the sun bespangled dome,
    Where floating worlds and centred suns are free;
Where rosy light illumes chaotic gloom,
    And fills the chambers of immensity!

Oh, peerless light! that gilds the sunny peaks
    Of yonder heights; that streams eternal
Hills with beauty!—whose ethereal freaks
    Phosphoric shine, making Nature vernal!
Thy ether ray pierces the ebon night,
    Where circling spheres and pleiades ever shine;
And penciling beauty with a fadeless light,
    Imprints the image on the sands of time!

Evanescent films!—the shades of Beauty's forms,
    Forever falling with fantastic grace;
Sweet emanations, shed by summer storms,
    In clustering splendor ornament each place!

Light flings her silver mantle o'er the earth,
   Painting the buds with tints from ether skies ;
Smiling the peering flowers into birth,
   Spreading her rich inimitable dyes !

Oh aerial bow'rs ! where lights forever pour,
   Shining Earth's budding beauties into bloom ;
Grasping the transcient glories ere they soar,
   Or reach the deep impenetrable tomb !
Sweet shades of friendship ! shall they pass away,
   When Light's soft touch could all their smiles retain ?
Shall forms of beauty perish in a day,
   When Light would bid the shadows still remain ?

WHAT IS HOME WITHOUT A SISTER?

WHAT is home without a sister,
What are all the joys of youth,
If in infancy we miss her,
And her prattling tales of truth?
Sweet affections may surround us,
And a mother's tender care,
But the magic fails to charm us
If no sister's love be there!

In her childhood, sweet affections
Spring around her spotless heart;
Hallowing each year reflections,
Prompting to the better part!
And when sorrow's deep emotion
Glides upon our stricken years,
Oh! what kindness and devotion
Doth she breathe to quell our fears!

Much we love a gentle mother,
Much we prize a father's tear;
And we love a kindly brother,
But a sister's love 's most dear!

Death and changes, never ceasing,
Oft our parents bear away;
While a sister's love 's increasing,
Growing stronger day by day!

WHAT IS HOME WITHOUT A BROTHER?

WHAT is home without a brother
For a pillar and a stay?
He can love beyond another,
And forever guard our way!
Words of peace are ever breathing
From those lips we deem so dear;
While his hands are kindly wreathing
Comforts for the household cheer!

What is home without a brother,
To preserve the family name;
That a father and a mother
May maintain an honest fame?
Love and goodness sweetly beaming
In his merry laughing eye,
Cheer the heart when tears are streaming—
Hushing up the bosom's sigh!

What is home without a brother?
One whose word the right commands,
And by whom a gentle mother
All the wants of age demands?
Loving sisters hang around him,
On life's rough and rugged way;
Tender parents lean upon him,
As their only hope and stay!

LITTLE CORA'S GRAVE.

I AM where the wild birds sing,
And their notes and tidings bring;
Where the spirit-voices ring,
'Midst the flow'rs that ever wave,
Over little Cora's grave!

Chorus—Oh! the birds will ever sing,
　　　　While their notes sad tidings bring,
　　　　And my tears flow like a wave
　　　　Over little Cora's grave!

12

Oh ! would she but calmly speak
To the heart that soon must break,
As I kneel and vainly seek
For the one I fain would save
From the sad and dreary grave !

I shall never happy be,
Nor from hopeless sorrow free,
Till that angel form I see,
Where no weeping willows wave,
Far away from Cora's grave !

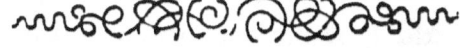

WILT THOU BE TRUE TO ME?

WHEN distant hands and distant hearts
　Thy fleeting hours beguile,
And winning beauty there imparts
　A fascinating smile;
When tempting pleasures there are found,
　Far, far beyond the sea,
And fairy joys your heart surround,
　Wilt thou be true to me?

Wilt thou be true in distant lands,
　If Fate should bid thee leave?
Will thy uplifted heart and hands,
　Forever to me cleave?
Should Fortune ever prove unkind,
　Or ever smile on thee,
In shade or sunshine, wilt thou mind—
　Wilt thou be true to me?

When thou art gone, far, far away,
　I 'll watch the star's bright beam,
And think I see thee in the ray,
　And ever of thee dream!

For thou, to me, art dear indeed,
  My soul cleaves close to thee;
My all in pleasure, pain and need—
  Wilt thou be true to me?

I 'LL BE TRUE TO THEE.

WHEN I am gone, and thou art left
  In this wide world alone;
From every smile of mine bereft
  That truthfully hath shone,
Believe me then to be sincere,
  As thou art true to me;
In pain and pleasure thou art dear,
  And I 'll be true to thee!

And should my wandering footsteps lead
  To Fame or Wealth's domain,
O'er deserts, or o'er verdant mead,
  I ever true remain!
No fault of thine shall ever turn
  That love that dwells in me;
Nor jealousy my spirit burn,
  For I 'll be true to thee!

Contented love has but one choice,
 One heart, her constant care,
For this she only lifts her voice,
 Which none with her can share!
Believe me then to be sincere,
 As thou art true to me;
In pain or pleasure thou art dear,
 And I 'll be true to thee!

SWEET EVELEEN.

THERE'S a sweet little cottage by the rolling river's side,
 Where the trees and the meadows ever green,
Laugh in the sunny glitter, as the waters onward glide,
 By the cottage of my Sweet Eveleen!

Chorus :—
O! my Sweet Eveleen, by the meadows ever green,
 Where the flowing merry waters onward glide,
Shall I never more be seen, in the summer's sunny sheen,
 With my Sweet Eveleen by my side?

How well do I remember the secluded little door,
    With its roses and tangled ivy green,
That crept around its arches and that sheltered from the shore
    The loved cottage of my Sweet Eveleen !

Many winged years have gone since I saw that little nook,
    Where we sat by the evening's starry sheen,
While the Nightingale would sing with the music of the brook,
    By the cottage of my Sweet Eveleen !

Thus the years have fled away while I've wandered forth alone,
    But in visions I see thee by my side,
And I cherish yet the dream, though life's tide has nearly
    That my Sweet Eveleen is my bride !   [flown,

TAKE THINE EASE.

Now Winter's blust'ring storms are gone,
And furious gales are over blown,—
Now sprightly Spring has passed away,
And Summer's sun with fiery ray
O'er Nature rules with burning sway,—
　　　　Take thine ease.

Now Winter's anxious care and toil,
With long, long nights of deep turmoil,
Has pass'd in Spring's more genial hours,
And April eyes have wept their show'rs,
And brought forth summers rosy bow'rs,—
　　　　Take thine ease.

Now Winter's hoary, fringy frost,
And snow-capped hills their gems have lost,—
Now hearty laughing, dancing Spring,
Has made the merry mountains ring,
And June-birds chanting, sweetly sing,—
　　　　Take thine ease.

Now woodland, meadow, hill and dale,
With violets, rose, and lily pale,
On downy ether, fragrance sweet,
Fling forth their joys thy sense to greet,
From busy world make thy retreat,—
                    Take thine ease.

Now richly laden fruitful trees,
In Summer's golden beauty please,—
Now rippling, purely vocal brooks,
Invite from toil to sylvan nooks,
And smiling Nature tempting looks—
                    Take thine ease.

Now Summer's carnival draws near,
And beast in playful gambols rear,—
Now lovely sporting fountains play,
And Nightingales with mellow lay,
Pour forth to stars at close of day,—
                    Take thine ease.

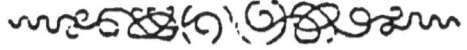

HOPE'S FLIGHT.

On, sunny heights ! illimited domain,
　　Where floating spheres and sapphire suns are free
Where Fancy wings, the topmost star to gain,
　　And scans the wonders of immensity !

Wing-poised she floats o'er spheres of ebon gloom,
　　To ether seas where Pleiades ever shine ;
And basking 'neath the sun-bespangled dome,
　　Her pinions fold, 'mid peerless rays divine !

Oh; fairy spark ! the life-lamp of the soul,
　　Thy upward flight reaches eternal day ;
Nor will thou rest till distant spirits call,
　　And bid thee all their glories to survey !

All past and present themes for thee are dull,
　　And would but limit thy wild, airy scope ;
The future only fills thy chalice full—
　　Infinite cycles are the themes of Hope !

Ethereal plains, of undiscovered bliss,
　　Still wait beyond our Hope's most distant flight ;
And shoreless seas, whose waves would ever kiss
　　The peaceful feet that love their fadeless light!

Unbounded Hope! what hand thy flight can stay,
   Or brazen chain prevent thy upward course?
As swift as thought, and fleeter than a ray—
   Omnipotence alone can stay thy force!

THE SONG OF THE SNOW.

I AM but a fairy—just going forth—
   A phantom on gossamer wing;
I 've come with a song from the far-off North,
   And I 'll make the broad valleys ring!

I garland the vales, and deck the great hills
   With jewels of diamonds and pearl;
And weave a white robe for all the bright rills,
   And silvery banners unfurl!

A garb of immaculate white I spread,
   And festoon the gay evergreen;
And on the top of the forest-king's head,
   My dazzling crown may be seen!

I 'm an Angel of Light—I watch all day
   O'er the tomb of the shrub and fern ;
Till the breath of Spring and the Summer's ray,
   Their life-giving power return !

I cover the hills, I cover the dells,
   I cover the graves of the flowers ;
I cover the rose and heather-blue-bells,
   Till they rise in their floral bowers !

The sweet little lillies, down in the lake,
   Will sleep there contented till spring ;
They know they 're kept by a little snow-flake,—
   · The down from my flying wing !

I shelter them all from the deadly frost,
   I light on my silvery feet ;
I cover them till the Winter is lost—
   Till the sweet sunny Spring they greet !

A GARLAND FOR AGGIE.

I 'VE woven a garland to crown thy brow,
   A garland, dear Aggie, for you;·
I 've gathered the lilacs—and even now
   They are dripping with morning dew !
I 've woven the rose and violets blue,
   With the fresh and gay evergreen ;
And heliotropes sweet—and all for you,
   Dear Aggie,—our gay little queen !

I 've gathered the pansies, that dew-drops sup
   With their sweet little puritan eyes ;
And the mignonette flow'r, and goldencup,
   That bloom'd 'neath the soft purple skies.
The fuchsia I 've cull'd, with crimson lip,
   All trembling with joyous delight ; ·
And all the pond-lilies, that waters sip,
   And smile in the bright summer light.

The lilies shall garland thy pale clear brow,
   Denoting thy innocent smile ;
And lilacs and evergreens crown thee now,
   To speak of the joys that beguile !
The heliotropes sweet, that turn to the light,
   Will show where the heart should return ;
And the fuchsia and rose, vernal and bright,
   Will show how affection should burn !

THE MAID OF SYLVAN NOOK.

'T was on a happy summer morn,
　I wandered far away
Among the ripe and yellow corn,
　And flowers rich and gay;
The bright birds carolled sweet and clear,
　To roses by the brook,
Where stood the cottage of my dear,
　The maid of Sylvan Nook!

Her loving eyes are blue and bright,
　With eyelids like the morn;
Her beauty is of peerless light,
　A rose without a thorn;
A fawn-like movement speaks her grace,
　A love-laugh 's in her look,
Her artless soul beams in her face,
　The maid of Sylvan Nook!

A GOOD OLD IRISH HOME.

'T is a quaint old house, with ivy porch,
  Where the wild rose climbs the wall,
Entwining itself with ivy green,
  Perfuming the mansion hall!
The poplar trees and the elms are there,
  In front of the mansion door,
Who rustle their leaves and nod their heads,
    To welcome the rich and poor!

'T is a quaint old house, with ivy porch,
  A paradise of the heart;
Its memory makes the bosom heave,
  And it makes the tear-drop start!
A dear old home is the Irish home,
  A home that 's never forgot;
It lives, and moves, and breathes in the heart,
  We call it a "sacred spot!"

'T is there 'neath the calm and gray old skies,
  Where harp and voices unite,
Till Echo the distant valleys fill,
  With songs of the sweet twilight!

Ah ! there is the grave old matron still,
  That never will be forgot ;
And there are the smiles of blooming youth,
  In the old familiar spot !

A dear old home is the Irish home,
  For memory still recalls
The primrose sweet, and a thousand flowers,
  That bloomed by its ivy walls !   .
My hope would fail, and my soul would faint,
  No joys would there be in store,
My throbbing heart would wither and sink,
  If I could see thee no more !

THE SOUTHERN STATES.

WRITTEN IN 1855.

THEIRS was not Beauty in the days of yore,
When pilgrim eyes first glimpsed the rugged shore ;
When savage beast in lair and forest lay,
And savage man, more savage still than they,
Who, like their native land, no culture knew,
But as the desert flow'r spontaneous grew,
Abruptly rude, unpolished and untaught,
Sublimely wild, and fabulous in thought !
Here the poor Indian, steep'd in sable night,
Salvation saw, and felt the glorious light ;
Here the proud Chiefs, in humble accents prayed,
And on the Gospel shrine their off'rings laid.
Thus the wide waste, of mind and earth's domain,
To Freedom bow'd and own'd a milder reign,—
The fruitless heath, the marsh, and barren sand,
Broke forth in verdure and adorn'd the land.
    Ere this bright era, in the march of Time,
In splendor burst, with light and truth sublime,—
Ere Freedom rose, triumphant songs to sing—
Ere the gold Eagle spread her glitt'ring wing,—
All nature mourn'd.   In vain the purple skies
Their garments spread, in folds of golden dyes ;—
In vain did spring adorn th' extended plain,

And summer winds breathe o'er the waving grain :—
The fruitful trees in vain spread forth their arms,
For savage life such beauties had no charms.
    What glory then awaits that noble band,
Who dauntless stood first in a heathen land ;
Who braved the battle, and affliction's rod,
For glorious Freedom, and the cause of God !
For such, the Muses ne'er refuse to sing,
But from Parnassus wake th' enchanting string ;
From hill to dale th' echoing notes prolong,
And nature sings the universal song !
    Thy past career, as far as eye has scan'd,
Is fraught with wonders, glorious, sad, and grand—
Wonders of labour, toil, of peace, and strife,
Of war, and death by pestilence and knife !
Tho' fears and hopes the mind by turns employed ;
Tho' friends and foes the little band annoyed,
Through all their faith triumphant victories won,
Through life and death unrivalled virtues shone :
Thus the wild winds that bend the fruitful trees,
Their branches strain and shake the rustling leaves,
Tend but to spread, and multiply their fruit,
Increase their strength, to take a deeper root.
    'T is just to dwell on virtues such as these,
For diligence rewards us by degrees,
If for ourselves we labour and we toil ;
Still virtue shines, tho' shining through the soil.
To honest labour, and to toil belong

The just reward, and burden of our song ;
For if to polish'd life our praise ascends,
Shall we not praise that on which life depends ?
   Happy the man that reads thy pages o'er,
Muse on thy past to wonder and adore,
Observe each step successfully arise,
Recount thy deeds, whose glory fills the skies !
Thrice happy him who reads and imitates
Those brilliant stars that gemm'd the Empire States !
   Various the ways and wonderful to all—
A nation's birth—meridian—and its fall !
It's like a flow'r that buds in rosy spring,
Unnoticed first, a weak and trivial thing,—
Shoots from the parent stock—its leaves extend—
In summer blooms—and winter brings it's end.
Empires, like seasons, come and pass away,
Have spring and summer, winter and decay,
Subject the same to never varying laws,
That wheel the world and own the Great First Cause !
   What means to ends in every work combine,
Seems hard to judge, to guess, or to divine ;
For noxious things with which we most contend,
The work achieves and brings the wished-for end ;
A deadly poison, used in right degrees,
The life may save, and check the rash disease,
Evil and good in equal parts arise,
As light and shade, or colors mix their dyes,
Each by each the other's presence show,
And evil lives that good may shine below.

Thus have we seen in thy past short career,
Darkness and light, bright hopes and sullen fear,
Weakness and strength, victory and defeat,
A brilliant charge, and then a quick retreat;
Wealth and distress in every step we see,
Sickness and health, and all with life agree.

Then each successive step let us admire,
The innate kindlings of progressive fire;
Watch every spark that from the altar flew,
Behold them blaze by every wind that blew,
Till wrapt in flame the ether clouds arise,
Spread o'er the world and swell the boundless skies.

Hail, fairy land! where is thy equal spot?
Brought forth of Mercy and by Love begot!
By Kindness nurs'd—thy cradle Charity,—
By Wisdom taught—thy guard Philanthropy!—
Eden itself would scarce with thee compare,
Tho' untold glories dwelt and blossom'd there;
Yet, all the graces that in thee were found,
Adorn thy States, spread, flourish and abound.
How truly blest and honor'd is thy fate,
Distinguish'd by the wise, the good, the great!
Heroes and Counts thy humble courts have trod,—
Poets and Saints—to praise and worship God.

Here Saintly Priest before the altar spread
The Gospel feast, that heathens might be fed;
Here Wesley sang his sweet and heavenly lays,
And Whitefield taught the thankless heart to praise;

Betesda, too, ope'd wide her mercy door,
And gather'd in the orphan and the poor ;
Here the glad voice the barren desert cheer'd,
And sudden verdure on the heath appear'd ;
The sandy waste a fruitful plain became,
And mountains leap'd to hear of Jesus' name !

　　If present joys become our lengthen'd song,
Our lengthen'd joys will still our theme prolong ;
For plenty, pleasure, health and wealth abound,
And in their fullness close the States around.
As days and months and years keep rolling on,
Improvements come (and old ones they are gone),
As balmy youth the nerves and muscles strain,
Expand and grow and swell the purple vein :
So Time extends the margin of thy bounds,
Stretch far thy wings and spread o'er trackless grounds ;
Till forests, plains, and sands, and desert drear,
With temples raise, and towering fill the air !
Here in thy humble walks doth wisdom shine,
And literature with love and peace combine ;
Here halls of knowledge fill'd with ancient lore,
And modern science crowns the useful store ;
Wise senators muse in thy sylvan nooks,
And plebian youths pour o'er the classic books ;
The Flying Heralds—(" Maps of busy life,")
Record the signs of peace, or bloody strife,
Watch all the points of Wisdom, Commerce, Wealth,
Of Mercy, Justice, Sickness, and of Health.

And here the *Drama* and the useful *Stage*
Live o'er the past and act the by-gone age ;
Make vice more vicious—virtue more divine,
And call forth all the graces of the Nine :
Monarchs and queens of Egypt's ancient year,
And Rome, and Greece with glory re-appear ;
Here Shakspeare moves with all-enchanting art,
And wakes the joys and terrors of the heart ;
   Here Euterpe, and her sister Terpsichore,
Their graces show and bring the loud encore ;
Apollo, too, o'er all the Nine preside,
And round the stage the fairy sisters glide ;
While mellow tones still on the zephyrs float,
Then growing louder, swell the trembling note,
Till bursting rapturous on the tempest flies,
Spread o'er the earth, rebound and fill the skies !
   Pleasure like these demand our grateful praise,
(What pleasure sweeter close our weary days ?)
Here vicious taste and viler appetites
Exchange their place for virtuous delights ;
And learning thus the great reward of Fate,
Choose this from that, this love, and that we hate.
'T is well we thus should cultivate the heart,
And nature learn, by watching every part ;
See through the mask that fairest acts disguise,
Learn to reject, and how true worth to prize :
Thus in thy midst are means of every kind
To teach, restrain, and to improve the mind.

Here, too, Minerva acts a glorious part,
And shows the beauties of the glowing Art;
Restores the seasons, or the sainted face,
And on the canvas wakes each living grace ;
With magic brush transfers the ruddy glow,
Or on the plate the mimic likeness show :
In every sketch, or tint, or rosy line,
You see the glory of the art divine :
Thus sweet Raphael and great Daguerre meet,
And pour out all their wonders at your feet !
    Nor these alone th' expanding mind delight,
Science and Art, both cordially unite
In deep research in Nature's inner laws,
Effects observe and find the hidden cause :
Hence in our midst the healing arts redress
The ills of life, the suffering and distress ;
Affliction here a remedy will find,
And antidotes to woes of every kind;
In every form that pain and sorrow blend,
Here find a cure, a master, and an end.

SOUTHERN SEASONS..

WHEN Spring's soft season weeps her timely showers,
And clothes the plains and raising hills with flowers;
When summer's sun awakes the vernal leaves,
And fragrant zephyrs fan the balmy trees;
When Flora ope's the rose's purple ray,
And mocking-birds first chant the opening day;
When lucid sun-beams wake the India Pride,
And rainbow beauties crown her branches wide,
Then bud the wonders of the Southern face,
And untold glories glow in every place.

Not less her beauty as the seasons rise—
Summer augments and decks with richer dyes;
Ethereal clouds their mellow tints diffuse,
And o'er thy graces sings th' admiring Muse.
Thus when the verdant shrubs and groaning trees,
And waving grain inhales the spicy breeze;
When round our groves the rich and teeming soil,
With crowded fruits reward the planter's toil;
Or when the Squares and sweet Arcadian bow'rs,
And gentle dews awake ambrosial flow'rs,
Then come! behold! a Paradise indeed,
Where Flora reigns and Nymphs on roses feed!

If gilded scenes now tempt thy ravish'd eyes,
Turn to the South, and fairer prospects rise:
See, o'er the plains the silver rivers roll,
And laughing lakes now dance o'er sands of gold!

When Autumn comes and clouds of deeper dye,
With ether softness paint the rainbow sky ;
When warbling notes pour forth like syren-isles,
And golden groves in yellow glory smiles ;
Then cotton-plants their emerald tints display,
And snow-white fleece the bounding hills array !
When Winter's face the melting Autumn ends,
And Lapland's frigid, icy arm extends ;
When rolling seas in frozen fetters bound,
And fleecy snow-clouds drift and swarm around ;
When northern winds breathe forth the hoary frost
And icy Alps in ether heights are lost,
Come then with us the sunny South enjoy,
'Neath mellow skies, where Winters ne'er annoy !

www.ingramcontent.com/pod-product-compliance
Lightning Source LLC
Chambersburg PA
CBHW021125020726
47500CB00003B/926